minedition

A division of Astra Publishing House
North American edition published 2021 by mineditionUS

mineditionUS, 19 West 21st Street, #1201, New York, NY 10010
e-mail: info@minedition.com
This book was printed in January 2021 at Hong Kong Discovery Printing Company Limited.
3/F., Blue Box Factory Building, 25 Hing Wo Street, Tin Wan, Aberdeen, Hong Kong, China
Typesetting in Optima
Library of Congress Cataloging-in-Publication Data available upon request.

ISBN 978-1-6626-5040-6
10 9 8 7 6 5 4 3 2 1 First Impression

For more information please visit our website: www.minedition.com

Jane Goodall Pangolina

Pictures by Daishu Ma

minedition

I'm a pangolin, and I was born in a big forest in
a warm and cozy burrow. My mother named me Pangolina.
Every night she went out to get food, always returning so I could
drink her rich, warm, delicious milk.

On one special day,
my mother took me with her
when she went out.

I clung to her tail as she walked
slowly through the forest.

When she came to a mound
of earth she got very excited.

"Look, Pangolina,
it's a termite nest!" she said.

Then suddenly, out of her mouth shot a long thin thing that looked like a giant worm. It pushed its way into a hole in the nest, and when she pulled it back out I realized it was her tongue — and many termites were stuck to it, waving their legs.

She pulled in her tongue and swallowed the termites!

Wow!

"Ah! So that must be what makes her milk so delicious," I thought. I watched as she enjoyed a wonderful meal, shooting her tongue out again and again and catching many termites. It must be very sticky, I thought to myself. So I went close to find out — and I found it really was VERY sticky, and for a moment my little nose stuck to it and I thought she might swallow me, thinking I was just another termite. But of course I was too big!

Those were wonderful days. I was happy to meet other animals in the forest. There was Civet — so beautiful with the dark circles around her eyes and a handsome spotted body.

I was a bit scared when Wild Pig and her piglets came by, grunting and rootling in the leaves — but they were only looking for fallen fruits.

Once I was startled when a large creature –
a bit like a fox with wings – flew low over us.
My mother told me not to worry because
it was only a fruit bat.

Almost every night, Bat flew past us
with his pals, and we became good friends.

One day we saw a very strange animal. It walked upright on
two legs and it did not have scales or fur or feathers. I was frightened.

"It's okay," said wise Civet. "It is a girl, the young child of a dangerous creature
called Human."

The girl squatted down to look at us. She seemed excited and her eyes were kind.
I wasn't frightened any more. Then a loud voice called out. It sounded like "Ai,"
and the girl jumped up and started to run toward the voice.

She called out, "Coming, Mom."

I grew quickly. My scales got harder. I learned how to open a termite mound with my claws that had become strong and hard. And one day my mother told me that I was grown up now and I should go off and find a mate, and that eventually I would have a little baby of my own.

That was how it worked, she said. She would be sad to see me go,
but she had to find another mate herself. That was the way of us pangolins,
the way we had lived for thousands of years.

I was lonely, but I still had Civet and Bat, and the pigs and a lot of other animals who were my friends. And sometimes I saw the girl, who I had learned was called Ai, walking in the forest. Gradually I got used to being away from my mother, and life was good until one terrible day that I shall never, never forget.

I was sound asleep when I was awakened by a fierce barking
and the paws of a strange animal digging at the entrance of my burrow.
Voices I did not recognize shouted something and all at once I was pulled
out into the daylight with a strong stick. A man, standing so tall on two legs,
pushed me into a cloth bag.

I lay there, terrified and trembling, as I was carried through the forest. Two of my friends, Civet and Bat, had also been caught.

"This is Human," said Civet, who was older and wiser than me. "He does not mean to be cruel. He thinks we are just things that have no feelings, that we do not know fear or pain. He just needs to make money so he can feed his children."

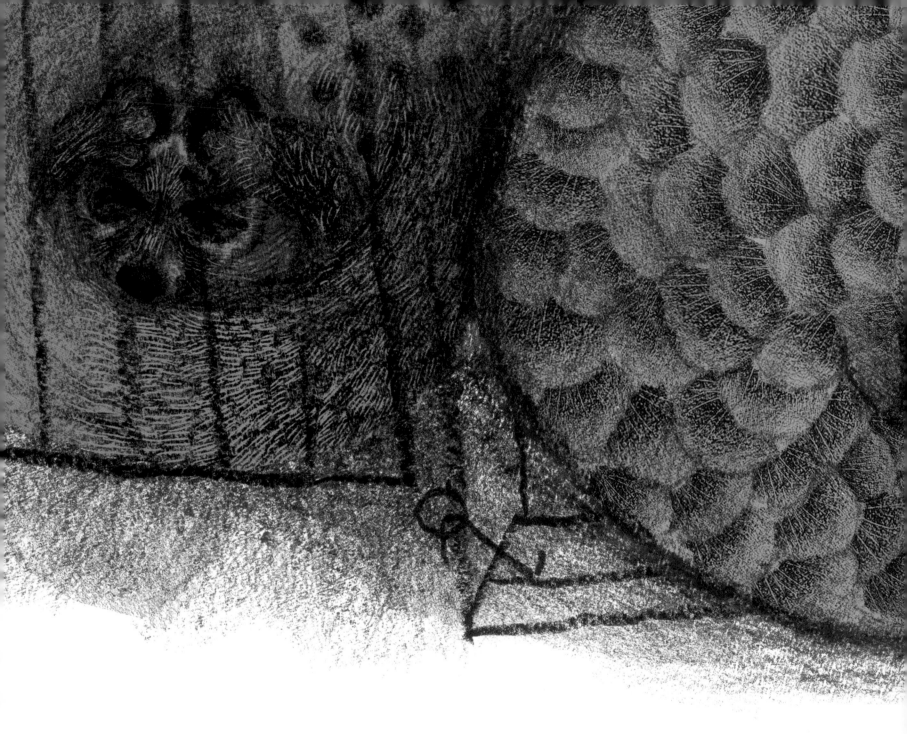

The man took us to a place where there were many cages full of animals
from the forest. Mostly they lay still and silent, but some were crying.
I was so terrified when I was pushed into a tiny, bare, and cold cage.
"They are going to kill us and eat us," said Civet, who was in a cage near mine.
"And they will pull off your scales because they think they make good
Human medicine."

I cried all night and I could hear the other animals crying too. And the next day there were screams of pain, and there was blood, and the smell of fear was all around me. In my heart I cried out for my mother.

In the evening I was pulled out of my cage.
"This is a good bargain," said the man who had caught me.

"Yes," said another voice, "I will buy it!" I was too frightened to move or even cry.
I just curled up into a tight little ball, as my mother taught me to do when danger
was nearby. Now I would never have my own little baby to love. I was picked up
and placed in a sack.

But then I heard a voice I knew. The voice of the girl Ai.

"No! No!" she was shouting. "Please don't kill her. I learned all about
pangolins at school. They are endangered. Look at her!
Look how frightened she is, Mom!" And she began to cry.
"Suppose it was me being sold for someone to eat. Someone
who would pull off all my fingernails to use for no-good
medicine. Please help me save the little pangolin."

Quite suddenly I was dropped to
the ground. I closed my eyes and
curled up as tightly as I could.
"Over there, over there!" someone shouted.

"I am a police officer," I heard another
voice say. "It is against the law to hunt
and sell pangolins."

The noises faded, and I heard small footsteps
coming toward me.

"You are safe now," whispered Ai.
I opened my eyes and saw her looking at me,
surrounded by many kind faces.

She looked at the police officer, who smiled at us.
"You must take the pangolin to a sanctuary,"
she told Ai's mother.

Ai picked me up gently and said,
"Let's take you to your new home."

Well, that was a long time ago.
Ai and her mother took me to a sanctuary
where I was safe.

And I learned that once humans understand that
we animals can know happiness and sadness,
fear and despair, and that we feel pain,
then they become kind, and care for us and protect us.

I will finish my story by saying that eventually I came upon a male. He was so strong and handsome and we fell in love. And so I got my baby, after all – a little boy who grew up and learned to feed on termites and make friends with the animals in the sanctuary.

People came to learn about us so they could tell more and more children about the animals of China, and how we have feelings just like them.

What a happy way to end my story.

Meet the Pangolin

There are eight species of pangolins in the world and all are endangered. Four of these are Asian – the Chinese, Sunda, Indian and Philippine. The other four – the Giant, Ground, Black-bellied and White-bellied – are found in Africa. The three species at most risk of extinction are the Chinese pangolins, the Sunda pangolins, and the Philippine pangolins.

Pangolins are the most trafficked species in the world: The International Union for Conservation of Nature (IUCN) estimates that in the past ten years, a total of one million pangolins have been hunted, killed, and sold. One of the reasons for the sharp decline in the number of pangolins is that traditional Chinese medicine holds that pangolin scales have medicinal value. Another reason is that pangolin meat is considered a delicacy, and to serve them to guests is a status symbol. Additionally, much pangolin habitat has been destroyed or degraded by human activities such as deforestation, the construction of cities and roads, and environmental pollution. Finally, their habit of rolling up into balls when threatened makes them easy to catch, and hunters train dogs to sniff out their burrows.

Mother and child

A mother pangolin gives birth to just one baby each year. The father plays no role in caring for infants. The scales of newborn pangolins are white and relatively soft. The color will gradually darken and the texture will become hard as they grow up.

When little pangolins are about 20 days old, mothers begin to carry them on their tails when they are foraging outside their burrows. They are inseparable. In the face of danger, a mother pangolin curls up into a ball around her child, protecting it completely.

At around the age of 5-6 months, young pangolins start spending time away from their mothers and eventually leave to start independent lives.

Physical appearance

Size
The head and body of the Chinese pangolin together measure about 35-60 centimeters, and its tail measures about 20-40 centimeters.
A mature Chinese pangolin weighs between 2.5 - 8.5 kilograms.
The male pangolin is bigger than the female.

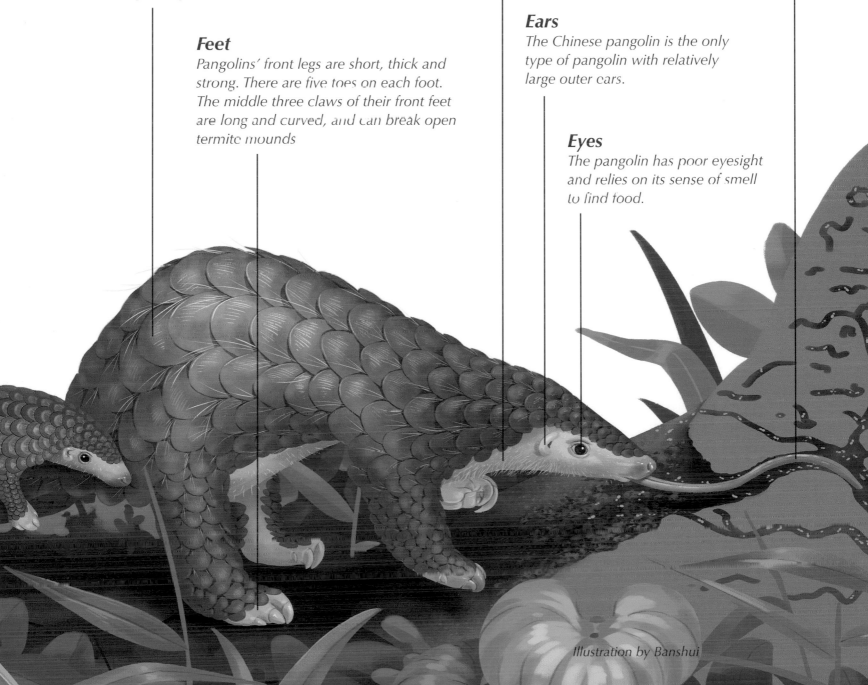

Scales
The pangolin is the only mammal with scales. The head, neck, back, side of the body, the outside of the limbs, and the dorsal and ventral surface of the tail are covered with scales, arranged like tiles, about 15-18 rows, with sparse coarse hairs growing between the scales.

Feet
Pangolins' front legs are short, thick and strong. There are five toes on each foot. The middle three claws of their front feet are long and curved, and can break open termite mounds

Throat pouch
When the pangolin is not eating ants, part of its tongue is hidden in the throat pouch inside the body.

Ears
The Chinese pangolin is the only type of pangolin with relatively large outer ears.

Eyes
The pangolin has poor eyesight and relies on its sense of smell to find food.

Tongue
The pangolin has no teeth and sticks its long sticky tongue into ant nests to prey. The tongue of a Chinese pangolin can be long as 23 centimeters.

Illustration by Banshui

Habits

Pangolins are solitary nocturnal animals (only ground pangolins are active during the day). They feed on termites and ants, and they have almost no natural enemies in the wild. Pangolins live as long as 19 years.

Defending behavior

Pangolins usually curl up into a ball when threatened. The English name of pangolin comes from Malay, and means "an animal that can curl up." With pangolins' strong scaly protection, carnivores such as lions and tigers can't eat them. The scales of the tree pangolins and the long-tailed pangolins are very sharp and can repel pythons.

The pangolin also releases an unpleasant smell from its scent gland when frightened, similar to but less powerful than that of a skunk.

Digging

Pangolins are very good at digging. The Chinese named them chuan shan jia (穿山甲) after this special skill. Pangolins dig as they search for food, and when they make burrows. But they cannot "drill mountains and make roads" as some people say, nor can they dig holes quickly in rocky areas.

Climbing

Tree pangolins, long-tailed pangolins, and Philippine pangolins spend all their time in trees, while Sunda pangolins spend about half of their time in trees, and giant and ground pangolins spend all their time on the ground. The Chinese and Indian pangolins seldom climb.

Swimming

Pangolins can swim. The scales on their bodies help to increase buoyancy.

photographer Zhou Jiajun

At present, the IUCN lists three species of pangolins as Critically Endangered, three species as Endangered, and two species as Vulnerable.

The Chinese pangolin is categorized as Critically Endangered, which is a degree of danger second only to wild extinction and extinction. It is two levels higher than that of the giant panda.

Despite this, we can still seize critical chances to rescue the pangolin. In particular, we must halt the expansion of human activities such as deforestation, road construction, and industrial polluting that have led to the continuous reduction and degradation of the pangolin's habitat.

Since July 2017, three Chinese pangolin Community Conservation Areas have been established in Hunan, Guangxi, and Jiangxi provinces. More and more people and organizations are engaged in the conservation of Chinese pangolins.

What can people do for pangolins?

1. Refuse to eat pangolin or buy pangolin products.
2. Remember: Pangolins are not pets.
3. Tell other people about pangolins and the importance of protecting them.
4. If we see pangolins in the wild, do not disturb them.
5. If we see pangolin trafficking, report it to the forest police.
6. If we discover an injured pangolin, contact the local animal rescue agency.

For more Information

Documentaries:

Pangolins: The World's Most Wanted Animal
Secrets of the Pangolin
The Pangolin Men
Looking for the Last Pangolin
Guardians of the Scales
Africa's Secret Seven
Seven Worlds, One Planet, Episode 7

Zoos:

Taipei Zoo, Taiwan, China
Vuon Quoc Gia Cúc Phuong, Vietnam
Taman Hidupan Liar Lok Kawi, Malaysia
Nandankanan Zoological Park, India
Zoologischer Garten Leipzig, Germany
Chicago Zoological Park, Illinois, U.S.A.

Websites:

Jane Goodall's Channel at BiliBili.com: **space.bilibili.com/662163337**
Wild for life: **wildfor.life**
WildAid: **wildaid.org**
World Pangolin Day: **www.pangolins.org**
WWF: **www.worldwildlife.org/species/pangolin**
National Geographic: **www.nationalgeographic.com/animals/mammals/group/pangolins**

Learn how our work is changing lives, improving outcomes, and protecting the world we all share:
www.janegoodall.org

Teaching Ideas

Public Service Advertisement Design: *Make a poster or shoot a video to show people around you how to protect pangolins.*

Thinking and discussing: *After reading the picture book, watch a documentary about pangolins together and talk about what you have learned and how you feel.*

Role-play: *Adapt the story of Pangolina into a script, assign roles, make props, and rehearse a picture book play.*

Creative writing: *Rewrite the story from another perspective (such as pangolin mother, little girl, hunter, or one of Pangolina's animal friends).*
How would Pangolina's life be like in the sanctuary? Let's write a sequel for this story!

Art Project: *Make coloring cards, finger puppets, clay dolls, origami, or collages of pangolins.*

A Philippine Pangolin pup nudges its mother, rolled up in a protective ball. Photographed in the forests of Palawan.
Philippine Pangolin Curled-up by Gregg Yan. The photo shown on this page has not been edited.
This photo is licensed under the Creative Commons Attribution-Share Alike 4.0 International license.
Link: https://creativecommons.org/licenses/by-sa/4.0/deed.en

THE JANE GOODALL INSTITUTE (JGI)

Only if we understand can we care
Only if we care will we help
Only if we help shall all be saved

In 1977 the first JGI was incorporated as a not for profit organization. Funds raised, through my lectures and donations from members, enabled me to continue the research at Gombe Stream Research Center.

From the start the mission of JGI was broad: to conduct chimpanzee research in the wild and in captivity, to improve conditions for chimpanzees in captive situations, to work to conserve chimpanzees and their habitats, and to create and conduct programs to empower and educate young people.

One of our most important programs is TACARE (TAKE CARE). It was initiated in 1994 to improve the lives of the people (in ways they wanted) living in 12 villages around GOMBE NATIONAL PARK. It now operates in 52 villages, and similar programs operate in Uganda, Democratic Republic of Congo, Republic of Congo and Senegal.

The Jane Goodall Institute is made up of offices around the globe.

The Jane Goodall Institute – USA Headquarters
1595 Spring Hill Rd, Suite 550, Vienna, VA 22182
Telephone: (703) 682-9220, Fax: (703) 682-9312

ROOTS & SHOOTS

Every individual matters
Every individual has a role to play
Every individual makes a difference – every day.

Roots & Shoots began in 1991 with 12 Tanzanian high school students who met on my veranda to discuss things that bothered them. And I persuaded them that they themselves could do something about their concerns. Each group chooses three projects that will make the world around them a better place – one to help people, one for other animals, and one for the environment. These projects can include such things as visiting the elderly, helping out at an animal shelter (or becoming a chimp guardian), clearing litter, or planting trees – whatever they feel is appropriate for their local area.

Today there are R&S groups in more than 65 countries, with members from pre-school through university, as well as an increasing numbers of adults forming groups. We reckon there are thousands of groups around the world. The collective impact is huge.

And, most importantly, members are empowered, ready to tackle the problems of their world.

The name is symbolic. Think of a big tree. It starts as a little seed. Pick it up when the first tiny shoot and roots appear. It seems so small, so weak. Yet there is a life force in the seed so powerful that the shoot, to reach the sun, can work through cracks in a brick wall and eventually knock it down. And the roots, to reach the water, can work through rocks and eventually push them aside. See the rocks and walls as all the problems we humans have inflicted on the planet, environmental, and social. And you realize R&S is about HOPE. Hundreds and thousands of Roots and Shoots around the world can break through and make this a better world for all.

There is a theme running through R&S of learning to live in peace and harmony with each other – breaking down barriers between nations, religions, cultures, old and young, rich and poor, AND between us and the natural world. There can never be peace if we continue to destroy our environment, as we are doing today.

Photo by Robert Ratzer / JGI Austria